Michelle Koch

HOOT HOWL HISS

Greenwillow Books
New York

Watercolor paints were used for the full-color art.
The text type is ITC Symbol Black.

Printed in Singapore by Tien Wah Press
First Edition   10 9 8 7 6 5 4 3 2 1

Library of Congress Cataloging-in-Publication Data

Koch, Michelle.
   Hoot, howl, hiss / by Michelle Koch.
      p.   cm.
   Summary: Depicts the sounds that animals make in the
woods, by the pond, in the jungle, at the farm,
and in the mountains.
   ISBN 0-688-09651-4. ISBN 0-688-09652-2 (lib. bdg.)
   [1. Animal sounds — Fiction.]   I. Title.
PZ7.K795Ho   1991
[E] — dc20   90-38484   CIP   AC

For
Holt

Hoot to Evie
Roar to Kris

Deep
in the
woods...

owls hoot,

wolves **howl,**

snakes

hiss.

Down by the pond...

ducks
quack,

crickets chirp,

frogs croak.

**Far
in the
jungle…**

lions

roar,

elephants

trumpet,

monkeys screech.

Out at the farm…

cows
moo,

pigs grunt,

hens cluck.

High in the mountains…

bears growl,

**mountain goats
bleat,**

marmots whistle.

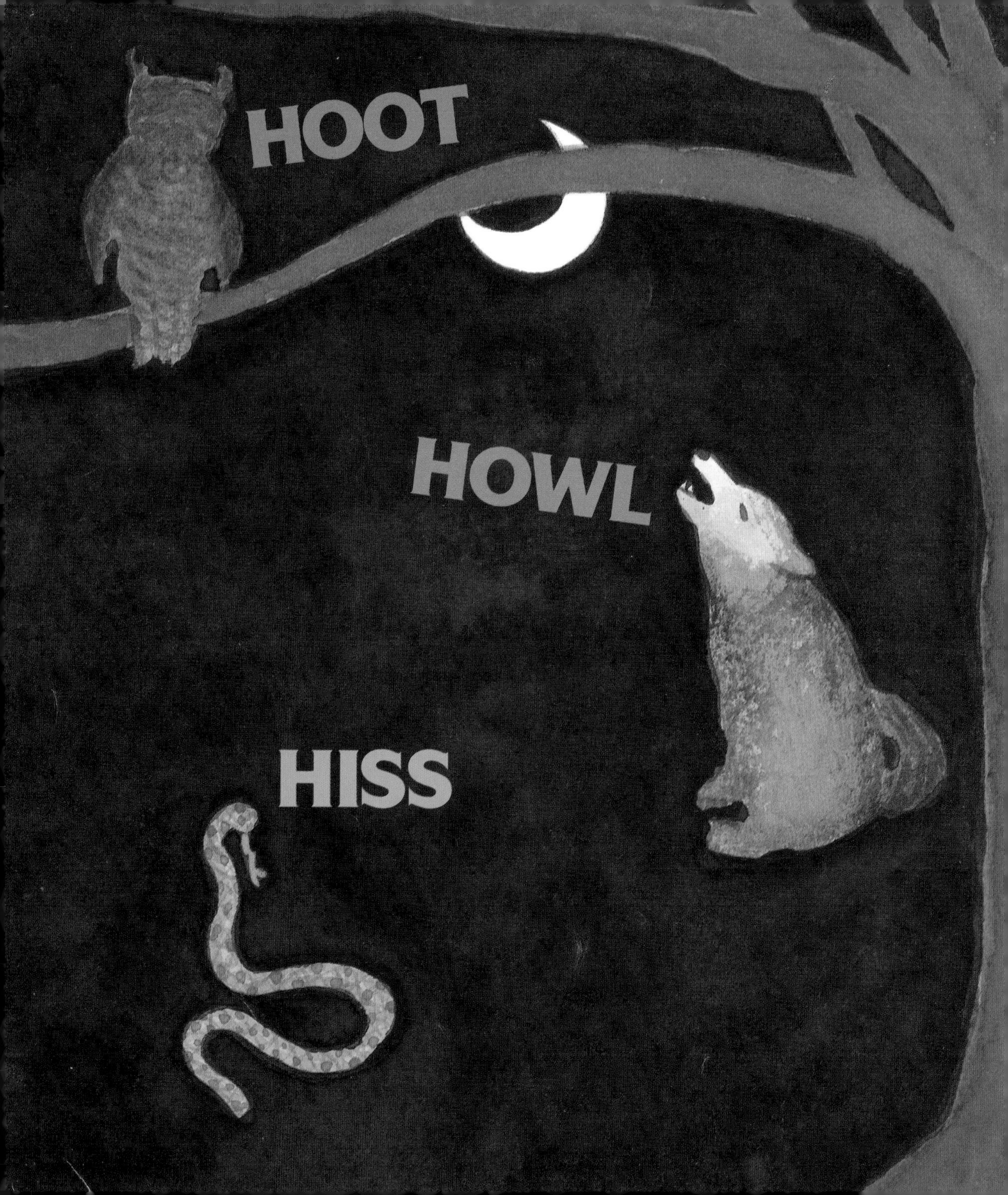
HOOT
HOWL
HISS